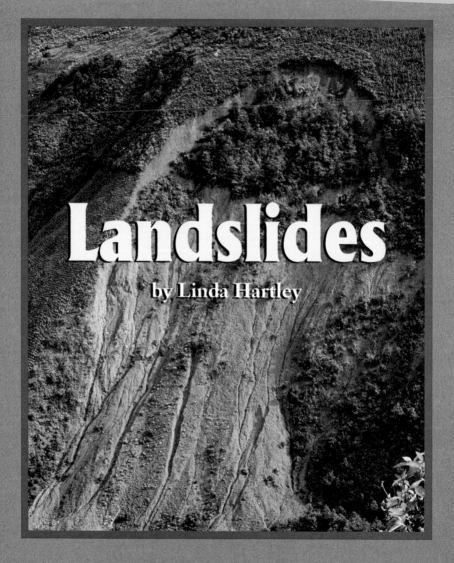

Landslides

by Linda Hartley

HOUGHTON MIFFLIN   BOSTON

A rock climber moves up the side of
Washington Column.

It was a warm July evening in Yosemite National Park. A rock climber slowly made his way up Washington Column. Suddenly he heard a CRACK! "That sounds like thunder," he thought. But when he turned his head, there was no storm. The noise had come from the side of a nearby mountain.

CRACK! BOOM! Giant boulders bounced down the side of Glacier Point. "I just stood there with my mouth open," the rock climber said afterward.

Later he learned that 162,000 tons of rock had rushed down the mountain. They had traveled at about 160 miles an hour. Fourteen people were hurt. One person died. The rock climber had seen a huge landslide.

Inset: A landslide roars down a slope.

4

A landslide happens when large amounts of rocks and soil move from a high place to a lower place. Visitors to Yosemite don't often see landslides. A long time may pass between landslides. But the work of landslides can be seen all over Yosemite — and all over the world. For millions of years, landslides have changed the surface of the earth.

The view from Glacier Point of Half Dome in Yosemite

Many landslides are caused by natural erosion. Wind and water wear away rocks and soil over time. Heavy rains and melting snow cause rocks and soil to loosen. If the land is steep, a landslide may happen. The landslide at Glacier Point was probably caused by natural erosion.

Before

These two diagrams show what happens during a landslide.

After

Geologists are people who study the earth. They know that landslides happen more often in some places than in others. Geologists look at rocks and soil and underground water. They measure slopes. They can often tell *where* a landslide is likely to happen. But geologists can't always tell *when* it will happen.

Most landslides are too fast, powerful, and dangerous to study in action. But there is one landslide of special interest. It moves very slowly, all the time. It is called the Slumgullion landslide. Its name means "watery meat stew."

Three scientists look down a landslide in the state of Washington.

The Slumgullion landslide in the 1800s

The Slumgullion landslide today

The huge Slumgullion landslide is in Colorado. Geologists can study how this landslide flows because it moves so slowly. Parts of the Slumgullion have been moving downward for 300 years. Like the fast landslide at Yosemite, this slow landslide is also caused by natural erosion.

Geologists use maps and photos to study landslides like the Slumgullion. Maps are made with the help of satellites circling the earth. Photos are taken from airplanes. Today's photos and maps are compared with old photos and maps. Geologists can see how the land has been changed.

Some landslides are caused by volcanoes. When a volcano erupts, tons of rocks and dirt can go flying down its sides. The volcano's power can create huge, deadly landslides.

In 1980 the Mount Saint Helens volcano in Washington erupted. A side of the mountain broke away in a great explosion. Lava and hot gases poured out. Ash, rocks, and soil formed a mighty landslide. It tore down millions of trees. Everything in the landslide's path was destroyed.

The Mount Saint Helens volcano erupting in 1980

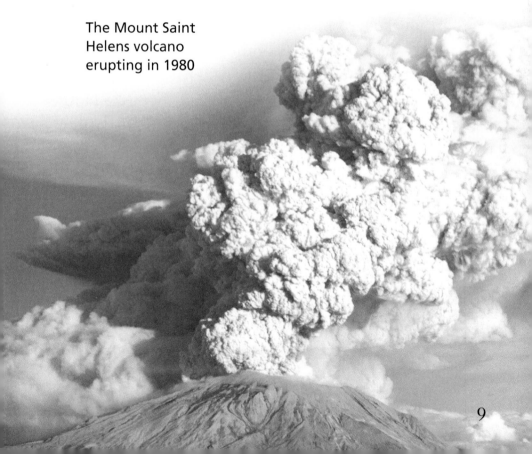

The Mount Saint Helens landslide seemed huge when it happened. But a landslide more than six times as large has been found underwater in the Atlantic Ocean. It happened many thousands of years ago. Its cause was an underwater volcano.

Underwater volcanoes have caused the largest landslides ever found. In the Pacific Ocean near Hawaii, scientists have found huge rock slides. Some of the rocks have moved over 100 miles from the volcanic mountain where they first fell. How did a landslide travel so far underwater? Scientists are still trying to find out.

Earthquakes are another force that can set off landslides. When large parts of the earth suddenly move, everything on the surface moves too. That is what happens in an earthquake. Rocks and soil are pushed loose from cliffs, roadsides, and slopes. All this stuff goes falling down as landslides.

The landslides caused by earthquakes are very powerful. In Montana in 1959, an earthquake caused an entire mountainside to slide into the Madison River.

By looking closely at areas where earthquakes often happen, geologists try to make predictions about landslides. They usually can tell where landslides are likely to happen in earthquake zones.

This gigantic crack in the earth was caused by an earthquake.
The same power can cause large landslides.

Large fences are used to keep landslides from falling onto roads.

Natural erosion, volcanoes, and earthquakes all cause landslides. Some landslides, however, have a different cause — people. When people change the surface of the earth, landslides are often the result.

Landslides are possible on the sides of many roads because of the way the roads were built. Workers blast away hills to build roads. The blasting leaves steep slopes. The steeper the slopes, the greater the chance that rocks and soil will fall in a landslide. Road signs that say "Watch Out for Falling Rock" warn of the chance of a landslide.

Nowadays, road builders can do several things to prevent landslides. Sometimes they fix rocks in place with large bolts. Sometimes they use wire fences to keep falling rocks from landing on the road below. The important thing is to stop the rocks before they fall.

Clear-cutting can leave huge areas without trees.

Another way people cause landslides is by clear-cutting. Clear-cutting is the chopping down of all the trees in one area. This gets rid of the tree roots that once held rocks and soil in place. Without the roots, rain can then wash rocks and soil down slopes in a landslide. In Oregon, many people believe that landslides are getting worse because there is too much clear-cutting.

Landslides can be a big danger to houses built near hills. Many people enjoy living with beautiful views, so they live in houses on top of hills. But if a landslide happens, the ground can come out from under these homes. They can go sliding downhill. Or a landslide can send tons of rocks crashing down on houses at the bottom of hills.

Builders are finding new, safer ways to build near hills. They cut back into hillsides. Then they remove the loose rocks and soil that could slide into houses.

The houses on the side of this hill in Hollywood, California, could come crashing down if a landslide were to happen.

When engineers and builders make plans, they study the land. They get helpful information from geologists about where landslides might happen. They can then decide where to build — or not to build — roads, hospitals, homes, and schools.

As builders clear land for houses, the safest sites get used first. Before long, houses are built on areas that aren't safe. But geologists warn that some places are just too dangerous for building. Landslides can bury a house in moments. Even a beautiful view isn't worth being buried in a landslide.

The giant mudslide in the photo on the right ripped apart homes on this hill in California.

Geologists are always looking for new ways to study landslides. They get better at predicting where and when landslides might happen. By keeping track of landslides, geologists can protect people from these dangerous natural events.

A giant landslide at Red Mountain in the San Juan Mountains of Colorado

Some landslides are caused by changes people make to the earth's surface. Most are caused by erosion, volcanoes, and earthquakes. Either way, landslides are both terrible disasters and thrilling events that shape our ever-changing world.